Forget It!

Julie Mitchell
Illustrated by Martin Bailey

Rigby

Contents

Chapter 1

Banned

"Hayley, would you please keep an eye on your little sister for me? I'm going outside to water the plants."

"Sure, Dad," I said.

Meg was watching TV, and I didn't think watching her would be a problem.

I was wrong about that.

A few minutes later, Meg was bored with the TV. "Will you read to me, Hayley?" she asked.

By then I was playing *Treasure Hunt* on the computer, and I didn't want to lose my man. "Sorry. I can't, Meg," I said. "Just get a book and look at the pictures."

That didn't keep her busy for long. Soon she was standing next to me. "What can I do now?"

"I don't know," I said, trying to escape the crocodiles. "Go and look at the fish."

Suddenly, the screen flashed. "Thanks, Meg," I muttered. "You just made me get eaten."

Meg went over to the fish tank and began to sing.

"Cut it out," I told her. "I can't think with all that noise."

"The fish like it when I sing to them! It makes them happy."

The screen flashed again, and I lost my second man.

"Great," I said. "Now I've only got one man left."

Meg came over to me and pulled my arm. "I want to play, too."

"Let go of me!" I told her. "You'll make me fall into the quicksand!"

Meg wouldn't let go, and my last man disappeared.

I lost my temper and banged my fists on the keyboard. I didn't know Dad was back inside until I heard his voice behind me.

"That's no way to treat a computer, Hayley."

I turned around. "But, Dad . . . "

"No *buts*," he said. "You're banned from using it for a week."

Chapter 2

A Great Idea

I tried to talk Dad out of banning me from the computer, but it didn't work. "You'll just have to learn to get along without it," he said. "A week isn't long. It'll be gone before you know it."

"No, it won't," I said. "It'll seem like forever."

At least I had something good to do on Saturday. My best friend Samantha had invited me to her birthday party.

The party was great. For a while, I forgot about my troubles.

Then, someone gave Sam a computer game for her birthday. When I saw it, I almost cried.

"What's the matter, Hayley?" Sam asked.

When I told her I'd been banned from using our computer, she couldn't believe it.

"Can't you get your dad to change his mind?" she asked me.

"Sure she can," Sam's big sister, Karen, said. She pointed to the tape recorder. "There's the answer to her problem."

"What do you mean?" I asked Karen.

"First you record a sentence telling your dad to forget what he said about the computer. Then you play it to him while he's asleep."

"Are you sure that'll work?" I asked her.

"Of course," she said. "I saw it on TV."

She turned the music off and put a blank tape in the recorder. "Just say the same thing over and over again. Are you ready?"

"I sure am."

Chapter 3
The Message

This is the sentence I recorded for Dad: "You will forget that you banned Hayley from the computer." I said it 25 times, just to make sure he got the message. Then I added a finishing touch: "Forget, forge-e-t, forge-e-e-t ... "

I took the tape home and dug out our old tape recorder. How could I sneak it into Dad's room?

My chance came during dinner. While Dad dished up dessert, I asked to be excused. Then I grabbed the tape recorder and plugged it in under his bed.

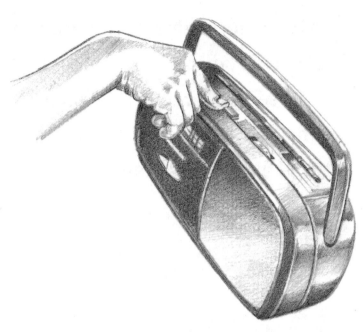

That night, I stayed awake until I thought Dad was asleep. Then I tiptoed into his room and crawled under his bed.

It was dark, but I could feel the tape recorder. I knew exactly where the "play" button was.

Carefully, I pushed it all the way down.

My voice came on right away, and I took off.

Moments later I was back in my room. When I was sure Dad hadn't followed me, I began to relax.

A smile crept over my face. Tomorrow I would be playing computer games again.

On Sunday morning, I joined the rest of the family at breakfast.

"How did you sleep, Dad?" I asked. "Like a log," he said. "How did you sleep?"

"Fine," I answered. Then I jumped right in. "I think I'll play games on the computer after breakfast. Okay?"

"Sure," he said.

"Hey!" Meg yelled. "Hayley isn't allowed to use the computer. You banned her, Dad. Remember?"

I held my breath. Dad looked at me, and a frown creased his forehead. "That's funny," he said. "I don't remember saying anything about the computer at all."

Chapter 4

Not Fair!

I couldn't get over it. The tape had made Dad forget all about my punishment! He didn't say anything when I turned the computer on. He didn't bat an eyelid when I loaded a game.

Later on, though, he started acting weird.

It began when he came into the living room, muttering to himself.

I turned away from the computer. "What's up, Dad?"

"I can't find my glasses. Have you seen them anywhere?"

I burst out laughing. "They're on the top of your head. You must have forgotten you put them there."

Something not so funny happened at bedtime, though. Dad promised to read me a story, but he didn't show up.

I waited in my room for ages, and finally, I went looking for him. I found him in the living room, watching TV.

"What about my story?" I asked.

"Sorry, Hayley. I forgot," he said. "It's too late now."

That was bad enough. Then on Monday, he forgot I was supposed to get my allowance, and he didn't give me any.

Wednesday afternoon was the worst. When it was time for me to go to gym class, Dad couldn't find his car keys.

"You always hang them on the hook by the kitchen door," I told him.

"Well, they're not there now," he said. "And I can't remember where I put them."

"How will I get to gym class?"

"I guess you'll have to stay home," Dad said.

Suddenly I was angry. "It's not fair! I'm always missing out on stuff because you forget things!"

Dad pulled a tape from his pocket. "Then maybe we should talk about this."

Chapter 5

Found Out

When I saw the tape, I knew I'd been found out.

"Should I play it for you?" Dad asked.

"No," I whispered. "I already know what's on it." I looked up at him. "You were only supposed to forget about banning me from the computer. Not about anything else."

"Sorry, Hayley," Dad said. "If you want me to forget about one punishment, I have to come up with another. It was the end of your tape that gave me the idea. Forget, forge-e-t, forge-e-e-t . . ."

I was shocked. "You mean you forgot everything on purpose?"

"I'm afraid so," Dad said. "Don't worry, though. You can help me get my memory back."

"How?" I asked.

"I'll give you a clue. It has something to do with the computer."

I groaned. "Okay. I won't go near it for a week."

"Wonderful," Dad said. "I can feel myself remembering things already."

"Would one of those things be my allowance?" I asked.

"Let me see," Dad said. "No, I don't think I'll be remembering that until next week. There's one more thing, as well."

"What's that?"

"When you're back on the computer, you might like to show Meg how to use it. Then she won't annoy you so much."

A week later, I did just that. I began with the most important rule of all: Never bang your fists on the keyboard.